Author's Note

On June 1, 1996, more than 300,000 people came to the Lincoln Memorial in Washington, D.C., to Stand For Children in the largest and most uplifting demonstration of commitment to children in our history. We came together as an American community to stand for what we believe in: healthy, safe, educated, and moral children. We committed ourselves to do more for children—as caring parents and grandparents, and as community, private sector, and public leaders. We stood together to say that our children must be our top priority as a nation and that no child should be left behind.

The Stand For Children did not end on that day, but marked the beginning of a new national movement to put our children first in everything we do. Today, Stand For Children Day is to the children's movement as Earth Day is to the environmental movement: a day to refocus and recommit to action.

You can Stand For Children no matter what your age. I hope you will Stand For Children not only in the beginning of June each year, but, even more important, each day and in every way.

Marian Wright Edelman
President, Children's Defense Fund
Convener, Stand For Children

MARIAN WRIGHT EDELMAN

quilts by ADRIENNE YORINKS

HYPERION BOOKS FOR CHILDREN

NEW YORK

We stood at the Lincoln Memorial as American families

and as an American community to commit ourselves to

putting you, our children, first, to building a just America

that leaves no child behind, and to ensuring all of you a

healthy and safe passage to adulthood.

We stood together as an American people—red, white, brown, black, and yellow; young and old; rich, middle class, and poor; female and male; physically and mentally challenged; Jew and Gentile; Christian and Moslem; Hindu, Buddhist, and Baha'i; believers and nonbelievers— each an inextricable part of the amazing sacred mosaic of God's universe and of America's democracy.

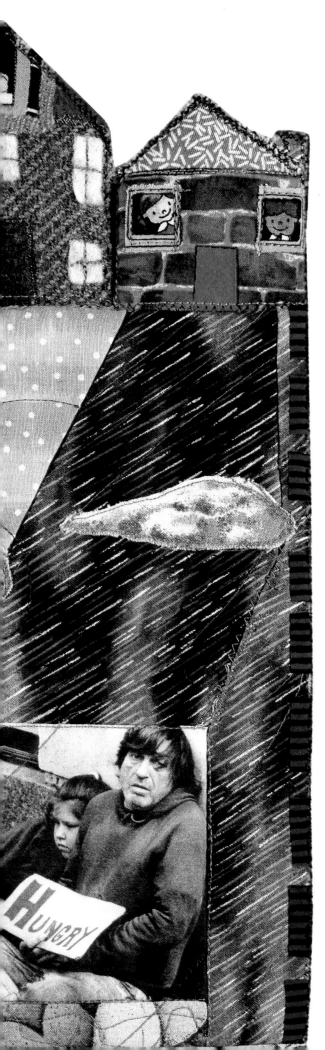

We came with many concerns and by many means for you, our children. Some of us walked and some came by wheelchair. Some came by rail, air, and bus. Some came alone and some in groups. Some came with family and some had no family. Some of us had one or more homes to protect our children from the cold, heat, and storms of life. Some of us had no home or place to call our own. No one was excluded.

Everyone agreed on one crucial thing: that no one in America should harm children and that everyone can do more to ensure that you grow up safe, healthy, and educated, in nurturing families and in caring communities.

You are entitled to your childhood, safety, and hope.

In this nation, the poorest baby born in the Mississippi delta, Montana plains, Texas barrios, Arizona reservations, and inner-city ghettos has the same God-given and America-promised birthright of fair opportunity, respect, and protection as the middle-class child born in the suburbs of Shaker Heights, and as the most privileged child born on Park Avenue.

Each and every American child adds or subtracts, multiplies or div

...erica's problems and potential, and fulfills America's nightmares or dreams.

President Lincoln warned that "a house divided against itself cannot stand." That's why we remember his words and are acting to renovate our divided and battered national house to make sure it has room and justice enough for all.

When Jesus Christ invited little children to come unto Him, He did not invite only rich or middle-class, male, white children without mental or physical challenges, from two-parent families, to come. He invited *all* children to come, as do all the great faiths, to renew America's and God's sacred covenant with every child.

It is always the right time to do right for children, who are being b

formed in mind, body, and spirit every minute as life goes on.

Young people, families, child advocates,

citizens: keep standing together for

children every day until all

America stands

with us.

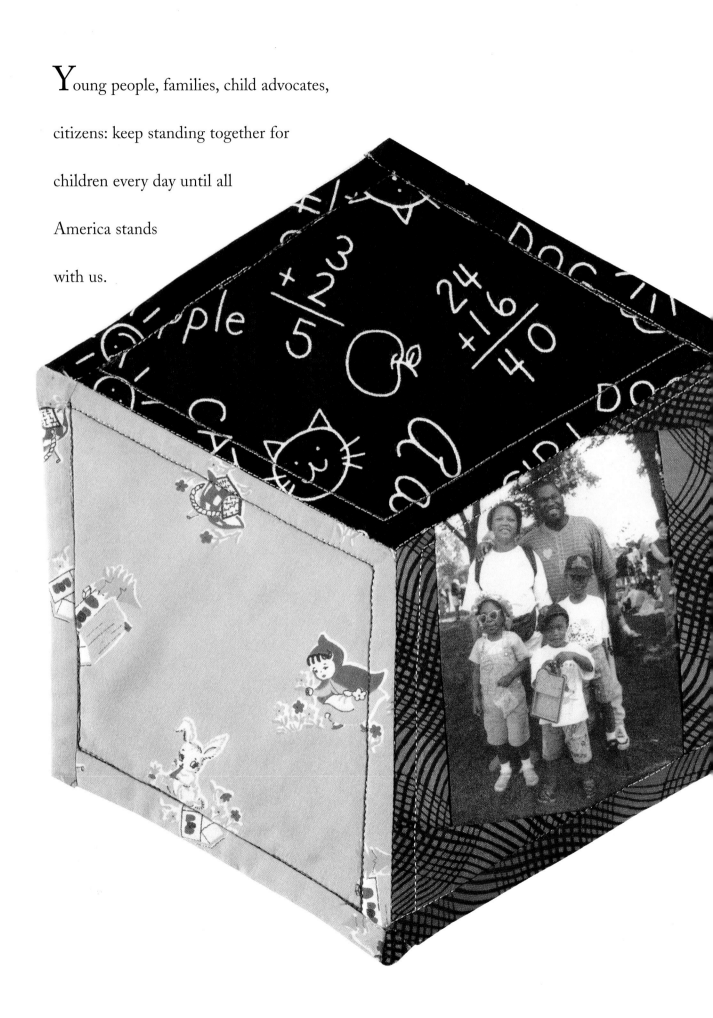

Take *at least*

one step for just one child,

and you will make a difference.

Be confident that you do not stand alone: we all stand together. We

He will make of them towering oak trees of hope in whose sh

our *very* best for you, and in doing so, leave our seeds of service to God.

can play and laugh and live and grow again all over America.

Whoever you are, wherever you are anywhere in America—stand up and commit to leave no child behind. If you cannot stand, raise your hands. If you cannot raise your hands, then lift your eyes or open your ears and hearts. If you do, you, our children, and this great nation will do God proud when He comes.

Trust in God's love. God lifted up Abraham Lincoln—a poor, rural Kentucky boy—to the presidency of the United States to save our Union from slavery and sectionalism. God used a courageous slave woman named Harriet Tubman to lead slaves to freedom on the Underground Railroad just as God can use you to heal our communities.

Let us end with a prayer.

O God, forgive our rich nation where small babies die of cold quite legally.

O God, forgive our rich nation where small children suffer from hunger quite legally.

O God, forgive our rich nation where toddlers and school children die from guns sold quite legally.

O God, forgive our rich nation that lets children be the poorest group of citizens quite legally.

O God, forgive our rich nation that lets the rich continue to get more at the expense of the poor quite legally.

O God, forgive our rich nation that thinks security rests in missiles rather than in mothers, and in bombs rather than in babies.

O God, forgive our rich nation for not giving You sufficient thanks by giving to others their daily bread.

O God, help us never to confuse what is quite legal with what is just and right in Your sight.

I Can Stand For Children

Here are some ordinary things that you can do to Stand For Children:

• Hold a yard sale and donate the proceeds to an after-school program.

• Start a bus token drive at your school for students who cannot afford transportation costs to school.

• Organize a winter coat and shoe drive for children in need, or go through your toy box and donate some toys to another child or to a shelter.

• Collect used children's books from your neighbors and donate them to a children's program or a child health clinic.

• Ask your church, synagogue, temple, or mosque to open the building at night for children in the community who need tutoring.

• Create a neighborhood garden or a container garden on your block.

• Write your state legislators and governor, your representatives in Congress, and the President to tell them to put children's needs first.

Printed in the United States of America.
Designed by Stephanie Bart-Horvath.

The text for this book is set in 12-point Caslon.
The artwork was prepared using various quiltmaking techniques including photo transfers onto fabric.

First Edition
1 3 5 7 9 10 8 6 4 2
Library of Congress Cataloging-in-Publication Data
Edelman, Marian Wright.
Stand For Children / Marian Wright Edelman ; illustrated by Adrienne Yorinks.
Address delivered June 1, 1996, at the Lincoln Memorial, Washington, D.C., as part of
Stand For Children Day.
ISBN 0-7868-0365-7 (trade)—ISBN 0-7868-2310-0 (lib. bdg.)
1. Children—United States—Juvenile literature. 2. Child welfare—United States—Juvenile literature.
I. Yorinks, Adrienne, ill. II. Title.   HQ792.U5E34   1998
305.23'0973—dc21   97-10831

To learn how you can Stand For Children®, call 202-234-0095
or visit the Web site at www.stand.org

PHOTO CREDITS: front cover: © Nita Winter Photography • back cover: © Ed Maguire / courtesy of Children's Defense Fund • author's note: © Jim Wells / courtesy of Children's Defense Fund
• pp. 4-5: photos of children: © Nita Winter Photography; Marian Wright Edelman photo: © Richard Reinhard / courtesy of Children's Defense Fund • pp. 6-7: all photos except photo of priest: ©
1997 PhotoDisc, Inc.; priest photo: © Ed Maguire / courtesy of Children's Defense Fund • pp. 8-9: children in house, clockwise from left: © Nita Winter Photography; © Nita Winter Photography;
© Joan Beard; homeless man and child: © Ron Chapple / FPG International, LLC • pp. 10-11: left, top to bottom: © Robert Maass; © 1991 Kathy Seward-Mackay, the *Nashua Telegraph* / Impact
Visuals; center: © 1997 PhotoDisc, Inc.; right, top to bottom: © Todd Weinstein; © 1997 PhotoDisc, Inc. • p. 12: top to bottom: © Todd Weinstein; © 1991 Robert Maass • p. 13: top: © 1991
Robert Maass; bottom: © Paula Bullwinkel • pp. 14-15: © Gordon Baer • pp. 18-19: © Nita Winter Photography • pp. 20-21: clockwise from left: © AP Photo / *Tuscaloosa News*, Neil Brake; ©
Paula Bullwinkel; © Nita Winter Photography • pp. 22-23: left: © Nita Winter Photography; right: © 1998 Earl Dotter, Impact Visuals • pp. 24-25: left side, top to bottom: © 1990 Rick Reinhard;
© Robert Maass; right side, top to bottom: © Nita Winter Photography; © Robert Maass • pp. 26-27: Abraham Lincoln: © G. Healy / The Corbis-Bettmann Archive; Harriet Tubman: © Brown
Brothers • p. 30: © Rick Reinhard / courtesy of Children's Defense Fund • p. 31: top and bottom photos © Todd Weinstein; middle photo © Nina Winter Photography • p. 32: © Rick Reinhard/
courtesy of Children's Defense Fund • Quilts photographed by Karen Bell.